Noddy is
Caught in a Storm

Collins

An Imprint of HarperCollins*Publishers*

NODDY

CLOCKWORK MOUSE

BIG-EARS

MARTHA

TESSIE BEAR

GOBBO

MR PLOD

MASTER TUBBY BEAR

SLY

ONKEY

MR WOBBLY MAN

BUMPY DOG

It was a gloomy morning in Toyland . . .

Noddy had just found out that his money box was completely empty!

"I must wash these breakfast things really quickly so I can earn some sixpences," he said to himself anxiously. "Otherwise I won't have any money to buy my tea!"

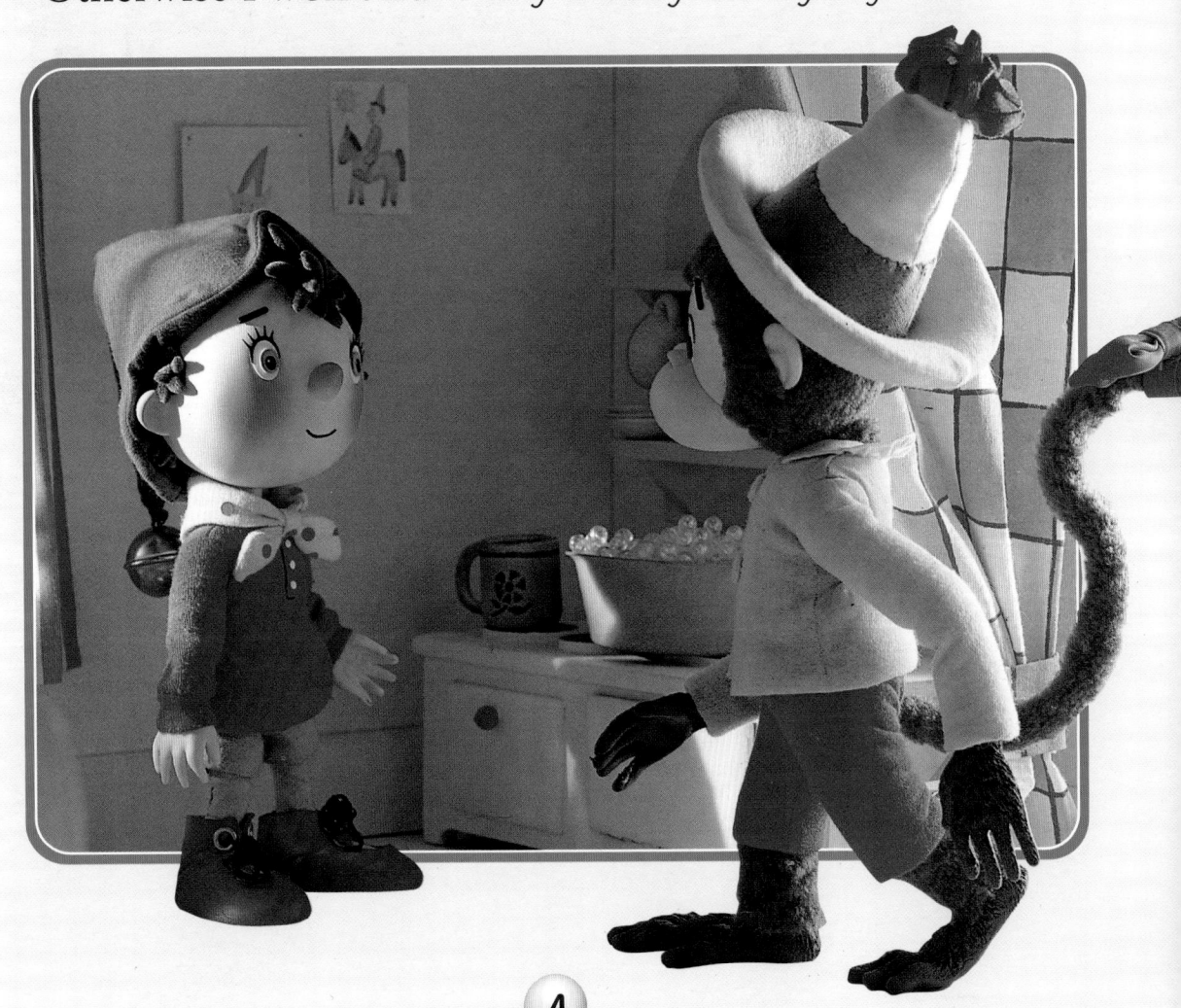

Luckily, a customer arrived almost straightaway.

"Good morning, Noddy," Bert Monkey greeted him. "Will you take me into town, please?"

"I will, Bert Monkey," said Noddy, delighted. "But you must pay me sixpence!"

"Bert, please try to keep your tail under control,"
said Noddy as he drove his car into town. "It keeps
trying to touch my hat."

"Sorry, Noddy," said Bert Monkey. "I think my tail
just wants to ring your bell!"

Bert Monkey tried really hard to control his tail but
again it suddenly flicked out towards Noddy's hat.

This time Bert's tail went right in front of Noddy's eyes.

"I can't see where I'm going!" Noddy cried.

SCREE-EE-EE-CH! CRASH!

Noddy's car smashed right into a wall!

Luckily, the car was not too damaged.

One wheel was very wobbly but Noddy was still just about able to drive his car to Mr Sparks' garage.

Mr Sparks examined the wobbly wheel, tutting gravely.

"I shall have to put on a brand new wheel, Noddy," he told him. "That'll take all day."

Noddy simply could not believe his ears.

"The end of the day!" he wailed. "Oh, when will I ever earn another sixpence?"

Feeling very miserable indeed, Noddy tramped aimlessly to the market.

Dinah Doll wanted to know why Noddy looked so sad.
Bert Monkey explained that it was all the fault of his
naughty tail. His tail had made poor Noddy crash!

"And now my car must stay in Mr Sparks' garage all day," Noddy said glumly, "and I can't earn any sixpences to buy my tea!"

But Dinah Doll thought of another way for Noddy to earn some sixpences.

"I need blackberries to make more jam. If you go into the wood and get lots of them, I'll pay you three sixpences," she told him.

Bert Monkey offered to help Noddy pick the blackberries.

So they both went off to the Dark Wood. And for once Bert Monkey's tail proved very useful.

It picked more blackberries than Noddy and Bert Monkey put together!

However, Noddy and Bert Monkey had no idea that someone was hiding nearby watching them pick their blackberries.

It was those two naughty goblins, Sly and Gobbo. They planned to steal Noddy's blackberries and sell them to Dinah Doll themselves!

Just as Bert Monkey was about to pick a big juicy blackberry, the goblins let go of a springy branch they were holding.

The branch flicked right into poor Bert Monkey and knocked him over.

"Oh Noddy, oh I'm stuck! Help, help me!" Bert
Monkey cried, calling to Noddy. "A great big branch has
attacked me!"

"Ha! Ha! Ha!" the goblins cackled with glee as they
jumped out of the bush where they were hiding.

"Thanks for the blackberries!" they chortled as they
stole the bags of berries Noddy and Bert Monkey had
collected.

"Come back, you robbers!" Bert Monkey cried out as he and Noddy chased after the goblins.

Noddy and Bert Monkey chased the goblins deeper and deeper into the wood. They chased through bushes, around trees and over fallen trunks.

But they couldn't catch Sly and Gobbo.

"It's getting dark," Noddy panted anxiously, realising that they were well and truly lost.

Suddenly, it got a lot worse for poor Noddy and Bert.
A thunderstorm broke out.

All the shadows came terrifyingly to life as lightning
flashed through the wood.

Bert Monkey really didn't like thunderstorms. He tried to hide away from the angry lightning.

Noddy didn't like thunderstorms either.

"We must try to be calm, Bert," he said bravely. "We won't get wet if we make a shelter!"

Bert Monkey did not have a clue how to make a shelter. Noddy was not too sure either.

Luckily, Bert Monkey's tail seemed to know exactly what to do. It picked up a fallen branch and handed it to Noddy.

Bert Monkey's tail obviously wanted to make up for all the trouble it had caused!

Noddy and Bert Monkey finally finished making their shelter.

They were only just in time because it started to pour with rain.

"Quick, let's crawl inside!" Noddy cried.

The shelter was very cosy but Noddy and Bert Monkey
were still quite scared.

The thunder and lightning now sounded as though it
was right above them!

They decided to hum a happy tune to keep up their
spirits.

Suddenly, there was a deafening crash, just above the shelter.

"The lightning has split that huge branch," Noddy cried, peering upwards. "Quick, Bert, we've got to run. The branch is going to drop down on to our shelter at any moment!"

Noddy was right. A few seconds later, the branch tore right off and crashed down on the shelter.

"Our poor shelter!" wailed Bert Monkey.

Noddy and Bert Monkey suddenly heard a faint *parp!* *parp!* in the darkness.

It was Noddy's car! As soon as Mr Sparks had repaired it, the little car had raced off in search of Noddy.

"My car!" Noddy exclaimed joyfully. "Oh, you are clever!"

Noddy's car drove Noddy and Bert to a strange little house nestled deep in the wood.

Noddy thought it looked familiar.

"It's Big-Ears' toadstool house!" he realised with delight.

"Oh Big-Ears, may we hide from the storm?" Noddy asked as his friend opened the door.

Big-Ears was very pleased to see Noddy and Bert Monkey.

"Of course you may!" he replied with a big smile. "I'm already sheltering..."

Noddy gasped on seeing the two naughty goblins in
Big-Ears' house.

"Sly and Gobbo!" he exclaimed. "And our
blackberries!"

The goblins tried to convince Big-Ears that they had
picked the blackberries themselves, but Bert Monkey's
tail soon put an end to their nonsense.

The tail started to tickle them both! The goblins just giggled at first but the tickling soon became more than either of them could stand.

"Please, stop tickling!" Sly pleaded with Bert Monkey's tail.

"Yes, get off!" cried Gobbo, trying to push the tail away.

Forgetting all about the blackberries, the goblins edged desperately towards the door and then ran as fast as they could away from Big-Ears' house.

Noddy, Bert Monkey and Big-Ears all laughed heartily as they watched the goblins run off.

"Well done Bert," Noddy chuckled, "Your tail really has made up for being naughty." And everyone started laughing again.

Even Bert Monkey's mischievous tail!

This edition first published in Great Britain by HarperCollins Publishers Ltd in 2000

3 5 7 9 10 8 6 4 2

ISBN: 0 00 136178 3

Reproduction by Graphic Studio S.r.l. Verona
Printed in Italy by Garzanti Verga S.r.l.

MORE NODDY BOOKS FOR YOU TO ENJOY

Noddy and the Artists

Noddy and the Bouncing Ball

Noddy and the Goblins

Noddy Tidies Toyland

Noddy and the Singing Bush

Noddy and the Noisy Drum

Noddy and the Treasure Map

Noddy and the Driving Lesson

Noddy is Far Too Busy

Noddy and the Magic Watch

Noddy the Nurse

Noddy Tells a Story